Kisses for Daddy

Frances Watts & David Legge

LITTLE HARE

To Nell,
and Frances Watts
—DL

Little Hare Books
4/21 Mary Street, Surry Hills
NSW 2010 AUSTRALIA

www.littleharebooks.com

First published in 2005
Reprinted in 2005 (twice)
First published in paperback 2006

National Library of Australia
Cataloguing-in-Publication entry

Watts, Frances.
Kisses for daddy.

For children.
ISBN 1 921049 30 8.

1. Bears - Juvenile fiction. I. Legge, David, 1963- .
II. Title.

A823.4

Designed by Serious Business
Produced by Phoenix Offset, Hong Kong
Printed in China

5 4 3 2 1

Baby Bear was grumbly. He didn't want to go to bed.
He didn't want his bath, and he didn't want to
kiss his mum and dad goodnight.

"Come on, grumbly bear," said his dad. "A big bear kiss for Mum, a big bear kiss for Dad, then bath and bed."

"No," said Baby Bear. But he padded slowly over to Mum and gave her a big kiss anyway.

"Now what about a big bear kiss for me?" said Dad.

"No!" said Baby Bear. "No kiss for Daddy."

"Oh," said Daddy,
picking up Baby Bear
and lifting him high.
"Well, how about a
giraffe kiss instead?"

"Baby giraffes give their daddies long,
tall kisses, like this…"

"No!" said Baby Bear.

"No giraffe kiss for Daddy."

"Oh dear," said Daddy, carrying Baby Bear up the stairs. "How about a koala kiss instead?"

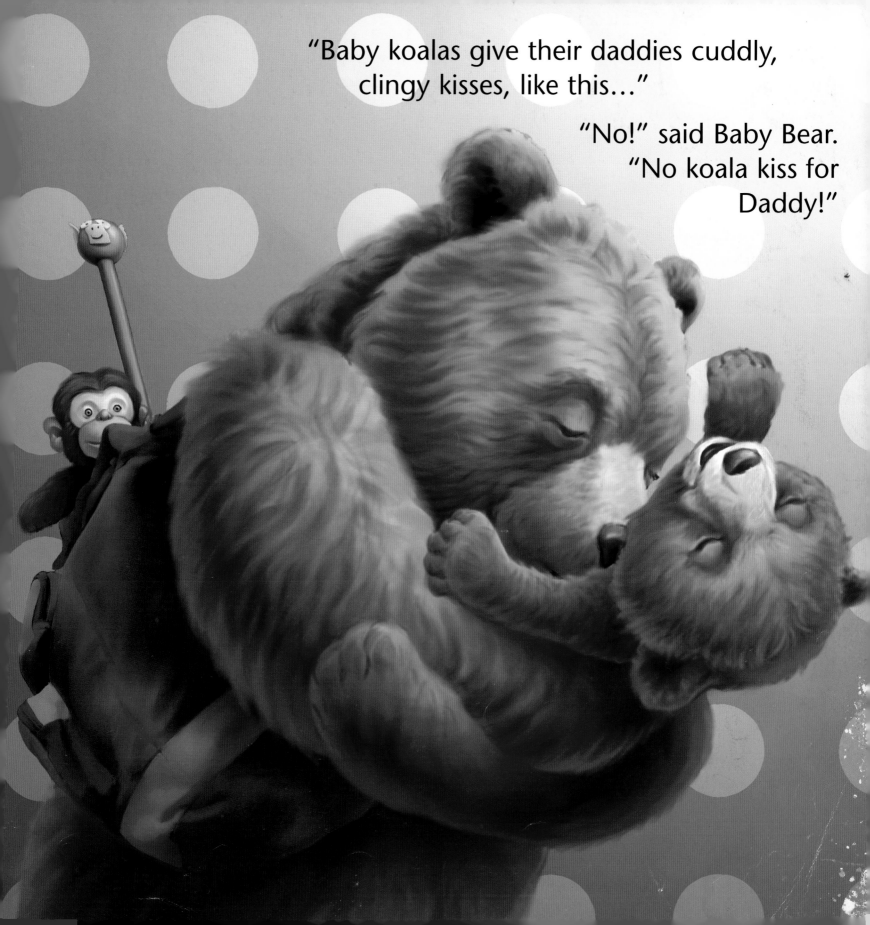

"Baby koalas give their daddies cuddly, clingy kisses, like this..."

"No!" said Baby Bear. "No koala kiss for Daddy!"

"Too bad," said Daddy, as he ran the bath.
"How about a crocodile kiss instead?"

"Baby crocodiles give their daddies snappy, watery kisses, like this..."
"No!" said Baby Bear.
"No crocodile kiss for Daddy!"

"Maybe that's just as well," said Daddy, as he rubbed them both dry. "How about a bat kiss instead? Baby bats give their daddies upside down kisses, like this…"

"No!" said Baby Bear.
"No bat kiss for Daddy!"

"That's a shame," said Daddy, as he gave Baby Bear his toothbrush. "How about a tiger kiss instead? Baby tigers give their daddies stripy, growly kisses, like this…"

"No!" growled Baby Bear.
"No tiger kiss for Daddy!"

"Never mind," said Daddy, as he helped Baby Bear with his pyjamas. "How about a monkey kiss instead?"

"Baby monkeys give their daddies jumpy, wriggly kisses, like this…"

"No!" giggled Baby Bear. "No monkey kiss for Daddy!"

"What a pity," said Daddy, as he
pulled the blanket up to
Baby Bear's chin. "How about a
mouse kiss instead?"

"Baby mice give their daddies tiny, whiskery kisses."

"No!" squeaked Baby Bear. "No mouse kiss for Daddy!"

Daddy Bear shook his head sadly. "No kisses for Daddy at all, then?" He sighed and started to walk away.

"Daddy!" cried Baby Bear.

"Yes?" said Daddy Bear.

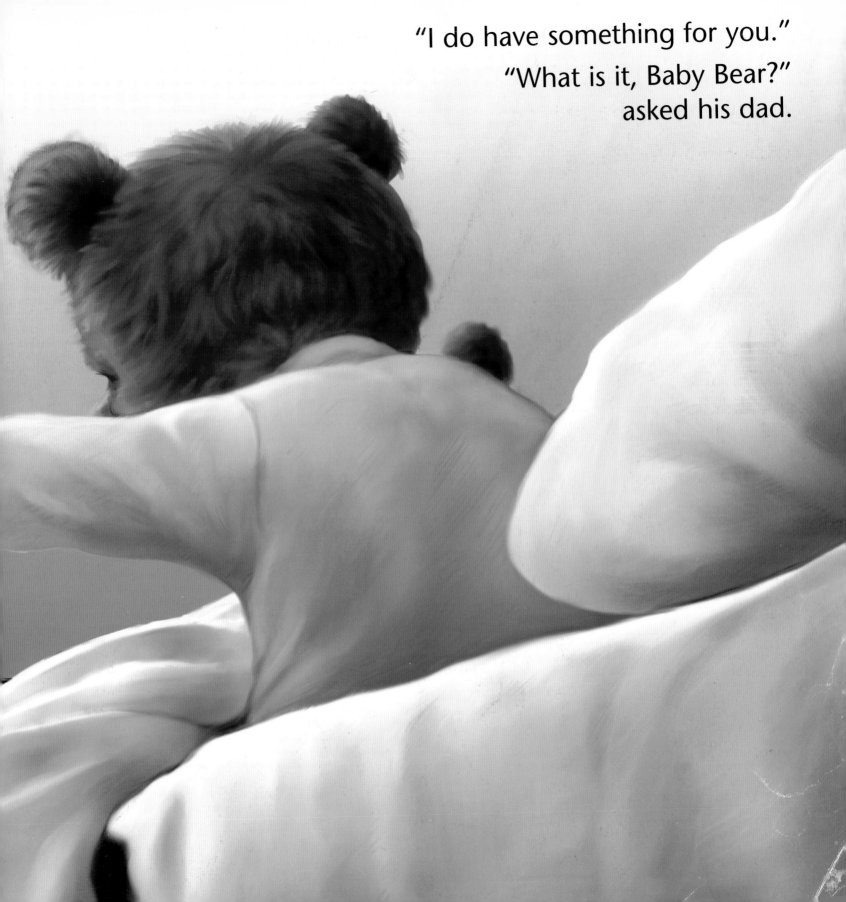

"I do have something for you."
"What is it, Baby Bear?"
asked his dad.

"A big bear kiss—and a big bear hug, too